The Hound of the Baskervilles

Introduction

Arthur Conan Doyle was born in 1859, in Edinburgh, Scotland. When he left school, he spent a year in Austria before studying medicine at Edinburgh University. He had to learn how to diagnose illnesses, and he later used some of these methods in the Sherlock Holmes detective stories.

Conan Doyle set up in practice as a doctor in 1885, but he still needed to earn more money. He started to write detective stories for a magazine. Two years later, *A Study in Scarlet* was published. This story introduced the detective, Sherlock Holmes, for the first time. Holmes, and his friend Dr Watson, became so popular that Conan Doyle wrote more stories about them. In 1892, they were all published as *The Adventures of Sherlock Holmes*. In 1893, Conan Doyle killed off Sherlock Holmes, but his readers forced him to write a come-back.

The Hound of the Baskervilles was published in 1902, the same year that Conan Doyle was knighted. It is one of his most thrilling and frightening books. It tells the story of the curse of the Baskerville family –

RETOLD BY PAULINE FRANCIS

EVANS BROTHERS LIMITED

Published by Evans Brothers Limited
2A Portman Mansions
Chiltern Street
London W1U 6NR

First published 2002

Printed in Hong Kong

British Library Cataloguing in Publication data.
Francis, Pauline
The Hound of the Baskervilles. – (Fast track classics)
1. Holmes, Sherlock (Fictitious character) - Juvenile fiction 2. Watson, John H. (Fictitious character) - Juvenile fiction 3. Detective and mystery stories 4. Children's stories
I. Title II. Doyle, Sir Arthur Conan, 1859-1930
823.9'14 [J]
ISBN 0237524023

a family haunted by a gigantic, fire-breathing hound that has caused many deaths on Dartmoor.

Sir Arthur Conan Doyle had many other interests apart from his writing – including the building of a Channel Tunnel. He died in 1930, at the age of seventy-one.

CHAPTER ONE

The Curse of the Baskervilles

BASKERVILLE HALL, Dartmoor, Devon

To my sons, Rodger and John Baskerville.

It is time that I told you the legend of your home, Baskerville Hall. It is a sad and evil story, but I must protect you.

Baskerville Hall used to be the home of Hugo Baskerville, a wild and cruel man. He fell in love with the daughter of one of the men who worked on his estate. This young girl feared him and kept away from him. But one September day, this Hugo, with five or six of his wicked companions, went to the farm and took her back to Baskerville Hall. They locked her in an upstairs room. Mad with fear, the poor girl climbed down the ivy outside her window and escaped across the moor.

When Hugo found that she had escaped, he was mad with anger. He ran from the house, shouting, "Bring me my horse and hunting hounds! I'll give myself to the devil if I can catch her!"

He set off after the girl. He rode over the moonlit moor, in full cry, like a man hunting a fox. His companions, sorry for what they had done, rode after him, to help the girl. On the moor, they passed one of the night shepherds.

"Have you seen the hunt pass by?" they cried.

The shepherd trembled.

"I have seen more than that," he said at last. "Hugo

Baskerville passed me upon his black mare, and there ran behind him the most terrible hound I have ever seen, a hound from hell."

The men rode on, cursing the shepherd for his stupidity. But soon their skins turned cold, for they heard the sound of galloping across the moor and the black mare went past them, her saddle empty. They rode on again, until they came to a dip in the moor. And there lay the girl, dead of fear and fatigue.

Then they saw the body of Hugo Baskerville. But it was not these sights which raised the hair on their heads. No, it was the sight of the beast, which hung over Hugo, a great black beast, tearing at his throat. It turned towards them, its jaws dripping blood, and they rode away screaming across the moor.

Such is the tale, my sons, of the coming of the hound which is said to have haunted the Baskerville family ever since. There have been many mysterious and bloody deaths in our family.

My sons, do not cross the moors after dark – it is a time of great evil up there.

Your loving father

Our visitor, a Dr Mortimer, put the letter back in his pocket.

"Do you find it interesting, Mr Holmes?" he asked.

"To a collector of fairy tales," Sherlock Holmes replied.

"And you, Dr Watson?" he asked, turning to me.

"I do not know what to make of it, sir," I replied.

"Tell me where you got this letter," Holmes said.

"It belonged to Sir Charles Baskerville, a dear friend of mine," Dr Mortimer said. "He died suddenly and tragically three months ago."

Dr Mortimer took another piece of paper from his pocket.

"Let me read you this now," he said. "It's the newspaper account of Sir Charles Baskerville's death."

DEVON COUNTY CHRONICLE June 14th

The recent death of Sir Charles Baskerville has cast a gloom over the countryside. It is only two years since Sir Charles Baskerville came to live at Baskerville Hall, but he had won the respect and affection of all who knew him.

The facts of the case are simple. Before he went to bed at night, Sir Charles Baskerville always walked down the famous Yew Alley of Baskerville Hall. On the 4th of June, the night before he was due to leave for London, he went for his walk as usual and never returned.

Mr Barrymore discovered his master's body at the end of the walk. No signs of violence were found. Doctors confirmed that a heart attack was the cause of death.

Unusual footsteps were found by the gate leading to the moor – "as if Sir Charles had been walking on his toes" said one policeman.

Sir Charles had no children. His next of kin is a young man called Sir Henry Baskerville, Sir Charles' nephew, believed to be in America.

"Now tell me what isn't in the newspaper," Sherlock Holmes said.

"I will be honest with you," Dr Mortimer said. "Over the past few months, Sir Charles had become more and more nervous. He took the legend I read to you just now very seriously. He never went out on the moors at night. He often asked me if I had ever seen a strange creature up there when I was visiting my patients. I remember one evening very well."

"When was this?" Holmes asked.

"About three weeks before his death," Dr Mortimer replied. "I was visiting Sir Charles one evening, and he was at the door when I arrived. I stood right in front of him, but he stared straight past me with a look of horror on his face. I turned round quickly and just caught a glimpse of something at the top of the drive – a huge black shape, like a calf or something."

"Did Sir Charles say anything?" Holmes asked.

"No," Dr Mortimer replied, "but he was in a nervous state for the rest of the evening. I suggested that he go away for a while, perhaps to London. But he never got there."

"Did you see Sir Charles' body?" Holmes asked.

"Yes," he replied, "his face was so twisted that I hardly recognised him. And..."

"And what?" Holmes asked.

"There were footprints on the path," Dr Mortimer said, "about twenty yards from the body."

"A man or woman's?" Holmes asked.

Dr Mortimer looked strangely at us for a moment, and his voice sank almost to a whisper as he replied.

"Mr Holmes, they were the footprints of a gigantic hound!"

CHAPTER TWO

The Warning

I shuddered as I heard Dr Mortimer's words. Holmes leaned forward in excitement.

"If only I had been called in earlier!" he said. "How can I help you now, Dr Mortimer?"

"Sir Henry Baskerville is arriving at Waterloo Station in exactly one hour and a quarter," Dr Mortimer explained. "I want you to tell me what to do with him. Is Baskerville Hall safe for a Baskerville?"

"But if there is such a thing as an evil force, it could harm the young man just as easily in London," Holmes said. "Go and meet Sir Henry Baskerville. Say nothing to him. Come back here at ten o'clock tomorrow and bring Sir Henry."

The next morning, at exactly ten o' clock, Dr Mortimer arrived with Sir Henry. Sir Henry was a small, dark-eyed man of about thirty, strongly built with weather-beaten skin. He held out an envelope to Holmes.

"I hope this is a joke," he said. "It is addressed to me at my hotel and bears the post-mark 'Charing Cross'. But nobody knew my hotel. I only decided to go there after I met Dr Mortimer last night."

Holmes opened the envelope and took out a piece of paper. The letters on it had been cut out and pasted on the page.

IF YOU VALUE YOUR LIFE
KEEP AWAY FROM THE MOOR

"Watson, have you yesterday's *Times*?" Holmes asked me.

I handed him the newspaper. Sir Henry Baskerville looked at me with puzzled eyes.

"Someone has cut out the letters from this newspaper," Holmes said. "I recognised the typeface of the letters instantly, and since it was sent last night, I was certain that it must be yesterday's newspaper. But the word 'moor' is not very common. As you see, it has been written by hand."

"Can you deduce anything else?" I asked.

"The handwriting of the address is roughly written, yet the *Times* is a newspaper for an educated man," Holmes replied. "This must be the work of an educated man pretending to be uneducated."

"I seemed to have walked into the pages of a detective novel," Sir Henry said.

"Has anything else unusual happened?" Holmes asked him.

"Yes, I've lost a boot," the young man said. "I put them

both outside my door last night to be cleaned and only one was returned this morning. What's going on, Mr Holmes? I think it's time you told me."

"I think Dr Mortimer should tell you the Baskerville legend as he told it to me yesterday," Holmes replied.

Sir Henry Baskerville listened in silence.

"Of course, I've heard these stories of the hound ever since I was a child," he said at last, "it's the pet story of the family. But I never took it seriously – but my uncle's death… and now someone wants to scare me away."

"There seems to be some danger," Holmes said. "Should you go to Baskerville Hall?"

"There's no man on earth who will prevent me from going to the home of my own people," Sir Henry said angrily. "I shall go back to my hotel to think about it. Will you and Dr Watson have lunch with me there at two o' clock?"

Holmes nodded and our visitors left.

"Quickly, Watson!" Holmes said. "We must follow them."

We walked from Baker Street to Oxford Street in a few minutes. Suddenly, Holmes noticed a horse-drawn cab, with a man inside.

"There's our man!" Holmes whispered. "He's been following us."

We caught a glimpse of the man's black, bushy beard

before the cab drove away at top speed. Holmes was angry with himself.

"I should have hired a cab and followed him," he said. "But I have the number of the cab – 2704."

We went on to Sir Henry's hotel to have lunch.

"I've made up my mind," he told us. "I shall go to Baskerville Hall."

"I agree," Holmes told Sir Henry. "Since you are being followed here, it will make no difference. But you must not go alone."

"Is it possible that you can come yourself, Mr Holmes?" Sir Henry asked.

"No, I cannot leave London," Holmes replied. "But I am confident that Dr Watson will look after you well. He will report back to me."

I was very surprised. Before I had time to reply, Sir Henry shook my hand.

"I shall not forget your kindness, Dr Watson," he said warmly.

When we were back in Baker Street, Holmes sent for the driver of cab 2704.

"Did your passenger give his name?" he asked.

"Oh yes," the cabman replied. "His name was Sherlock Holmes."

When the cabman had gone, Holmes turned to me with a smile.

"We end where we began," he said. "The cunning rascal. He knew what we were up to! I wish you better luck in Devonshire, Dr Watson."

CHAPTER THREE

To Baskerville Hall

It was dark when Sir Henry and I rode over the top of Dartmoor. A cold autumnal wind swept across it and made us shiver. Even Sir Henry fell silent and pulled his overcoat more closely around him. The road in front of us grew bleaker and wilder over slopes sprinkled with giant boulders. Suddenly, we looked down into a valley dotted with stunted trees, and saw two high, narrow towers.

"Baskerville Hall!" the driver called.

Sir Henry stood up and looked with flushed cheeks and shining eyes.

We passed through the gateway, then through an avenue of dark trees. Baskerville shuddered as he looked up the long, dark drive where the house glimmered like a ghost at the end.

"Did my uncle die here?" he asked in a low voice.

"No, no," I said, "in the Yew Alley on the other side."

Sir Henry glanced around with a gloomy face.

"It's no wonder my uncle felt trouble coming to him in such a place as this," he said. "It's enough to scare any man. I'll have a row of electric lamps here in six months."

We went to bed early that night. I drew back my

curtains before I got into bed and looked from my window. The trees moaned and twisted in the wind. And beyond, I could see the rising moor in the half-moonlight.

I slept very badly. In the middle of the night, a terrible sound came to my ears – the sob of a woman, strangling and gasping and not far away.

The beauty of the next morning did much to cheer us up. As Sir Henry and I sat at breakfast, sunlight flooded in through the windows.

"I guess it is ourselves and not the house that we have to blame!" Sir Henry said. "We were tired from our journey, so we found this place very gloomy. Now we are fresh and well, it seems cheerful again."

"But not entirely," I answered. "Did you hear a woman sobbing in the night?"

"Yes, when I was half-asleep," Sir Henry replied. "We must find out about this immediately."

He rang the bell and Barrymore entered. Sir Henry asked him about the woman.

"There are only two women in the house, Sir Henry," he answered. "One is the scullery maid, who sleeps in the other wing of the house. The other is my wife, and the sound could not have come from her."

I knew that he was lying when I met Mrs Barrymore later in the corridor. Her eyes were red and swollen.

Already there was an atmosphere of mystery around this handsome, black-bearded butler. He had been the first person to discover Sir Charles' body! Was he the man who had followed us in the London cab only two days ago? But what interest could he have in persecuting the Baskerville family?

As Sir Henry was busy that morning, I walked four miles to the edge of the moor, in the direction of Dr Mortimer's house. Someone called out, "Dr Watson!" and I turned round to see a stranger – a small, clean-shaven man with blond hair. He was about thirty or forty years of age, dressed in a grey suit and wearing a straw hat. He was carrying a butterfly net.

"My name is Jack Stapleton," he said, " a friend of Dr Mortimer. He has told me about you. Has Mr Sherlock Holmes come to any conclusion yet? And may I ask if Mr Holmes himself will be visiting Devon?"

"I assure you that I am here simply on a visit to my friend, Sir Henry," I said, surprised by so many questions.

"Excellent!" Stapleton said, "you are right to be careful. I shall not mention the matter again. Now come home with me to Merripit House and meet my sister."

As we walked together, he pointed to some hills in the distance.

"Be careful if you walk over there," he said. "There's a terrible bog just in front of the hills – Grimpen Mire. It will suck you down in seconds. I know a safe path through it. I often go into the hills to catch my butterflies."

A shiver ran down my spine as he spoke. Suddenly, a long, low moan filled the air. It became a loud roar, then a sad murmur.

"What is it?" I asked him.

"People here say it's the Hound of the Baskervilles calling for its victims," Stapleton told me. "I've heard it before, but never so loud. But I don't believe such nonsense. It's probably just a bird."

As we came near to the house, Miss Stapleton came out to meet us. To my amazement, she came up to me and whispered, "Go back! Go straight back to London! Never set foot on this moor again!"

I could only stare at her in stupid surprise until her brother joined us.

"I was telling Sir Henry that it was rather late for him to see the true beauties of the moors," Miss Stapleton said quickly.

"My name is Dr Watson," I told her. "I am Sir Henry's friend."

Miss Stapleton looked at me angrily and went into the house. I did not stay with them long. On my return journey, I came across Miss Stapleton again, sitting on a rock by the side of the path.

"I apologise for my stupid mistake earlier," she said. "Please forget what I said."

"But I am Sir Henry's friend," I said. "Tell me what the danger is."

"You know the story of the hound?"

"I do not believe in such nonsense," I said.

"But I do," Miss Stapleton replied. "Please take Sir Henry away from this dangerous place."

She turned and disappeared in a few minutes among the scattered boulders. And I, full of fear, went on my way to Baskerville Hall.

CHAPTER FOUR

Dr Watson's Reports

Baskerville Hall, Oct. 13th

My dear Holmes

Let me tell you about the strange events of last night. You know that I am not a very sound sleeper, and since I have been on guard in this house, my sleep has been lighter than ever. At about two o' clock in the morning, I heard someone creep past my door. I peeped out and saw Barrymore, barefoot and carrying a candle!

I followed him to one of the empty rooms at the end of the corridor. In the room, Barrymore crouched by the window. He put out his candle and stood staring into the blackness of the moor.

There is some secret business going on in this house of gloom!

This morning, I told Sir Henry what I had seen, and we have made a plan which should make my next report more interesting. Tonight, we shall sit up all night to see if Barrymore visits the room again.

Dr Watson

Baskerville Hall, Oct. 15th

My dear Holmes

Things have now become clearer and more complicated at the same time!

Yesterday morning, Sir Henry set off for a walk on the moors. He would not let me go with him; but when he had been gone some time, I decided to go after him. I saw him from the path, in the company of Miss Stapleton. Then a wisp of green floating in the air caught my eye, and I saw Jack Stapleton carrying his butterfly net. He was much closer to them than I was. When he saw them he seemed to be angry. His sister left Sir Henry and walked off with her brother.

I ran down the hill to speak to Sir Henry.

"Do you think Jack Stapleton is mad?" he asked me.

"I don't think so," I said. "Why do you ask?"

"He does not want me even to touch the tip of his sister's fingers," he said bitterly. "I want to marry her, Watson. I love her. But her brother is mad with anger. Why, oh why?"

I was puzzled. However, our minds were put at rest that same afternoon. Stapleton came to Baskerville Hall to apologise for his behaviour. He said he could not bear the thought of losing his dear sister. So that is one of our little mysteries cleared up!

Now what about Barrymore? We did not see him until the second night. He was crouching at the same window, just as before.

Sir Henry walked straight into the room.

"What are you doing here, Barrymore?" he asked.

"Nothing, sir," Barrymore replied. He was so upset that he could hardly speak. "I am making sure that the window is fastened."

"Tell the truth!" Sir Henry said sternly "Who is out there?"

"Don't ask me, Sir Henry – don't ask me!" Barrymore said. "It is not my secret and I cannot tell it."

"You should be ashamed of yourself!" Sir Henry shouted. "Your family has lived with mine for over a hundred years, and now you plot against me!"

"No, no, sir, no, not against you!"

It was a woman's voice, and Mrs Barrymore, paler and more horror-struck than her husband, was standing at the door.

"It's my doing, Sir Henry – all mine," she said. "He's done nothing except for my sake, and because I asked him." She paused. "My brother has escaped from the prison on the moor. Now he's starving out there. The signal is to tell him that there's food here for him."

Sir Henry was a kind man and he promised not to say anything more. But when the Barrymores had left, he was worried.

"The Stapletons may not be safe from this prisoner," he said. "Dr Watson, will you come onto the moor with me, and see if we can catch the man ourselves?"

I agreed and we set off into the darkness.

"What would Holmes say?" Sir Henry laughed. "Out on

the moor at this time of the night!"

As if in answer to his words, a strange cry rose from the moor, the cry I had already heard on the Grimpen Mire. It came with the wind through the silence of the night, rising to a howl, then dying away in a sad moan. Again and again it came, wild and terrifying.

"Watson," said Sir Henry, "it was the cry of a hound, the Hound of the Baskervilles!"

My blood ran cold in my veins as I heard the terror in his voice.

"Is it possible I may be in danger from evil?" he asked me. "It was one thing to laugh about it in London, and another to stand out here in the darkness of the moor and hear such a cry! That sound froze my blood, Watson!"

But he refused to turn back. We stumbled slowly in the darkness, until we came to a flickering candle stuck in a rock. Then we saw the prisoner, but he ran off as soon as he saw us. We ran after him until we could run no more. Then we turned back for Baskerville Hall.

As I glanced back, Holmes, I saw a man standing on a rock in the moonlight. Not the convict, but a tall, thin man. He stood with his arms folded, his head bowed. Then he disappeared, before Sir Henry could see him.

I wish you could come down to Devon, to shed some light on this.

Dr Watson

CHAPTER FIVE

Dr Watson's Diary

October 16th – a dull and foggy day, with a drizzle of rain. It is sad both outside and in. I feel that there is danger all around. Barrymore was angry with us for hunting his brother-in-law. We promised, at last, not to tell the police.

Barrymore was so happy to hear this that he told us more about the night of the murder.

"I should have said it before," he told us, "but I only found out a long time after the inquest. I've never breathed a word about it."

"Do you know how Sir Charles died?" I asked him.

"No, sir, I don't know that," Barrymore replied, "but I do know why he was at the gate to the moor. It was to meet a woman."

"And the woman's name?" I asked.

"I can't give you the name, sir, but I can give you the initials. They were L.L."

"How do you know this?" Sir Henry asked.

"Your uncle received a letter on the morning of the day he died," Barrymore explained. "It was from a village called Coombe Tracey. Sir Charles burned it, but I saw the remains of it in the fireplace. I could just read the last line… "Please, please, as you are a gentleman, burn this letter, and be at the gate by ten o'clock. L.L."

"Thank you, Barrymore," Sir Henry said, "you can go."

He turned to me.

"Well, Watson," he said, "what do you think of that?"

"It seems to leave the darkness rather blacker than before," I said. "I shall tell Holmes. He may come down here."

Oct. 17th

All day the rain has poured down, rustling down the ivy. I thought of the poor prisoner out on the moor and that strange man standing against the moon.

In the evening, I walked on the moor, the rain beating upon my face and the wind whistling in my ears. Heavy, slate-coloured clouds hung low over the hills.

On my way back, Dr Mortimer passed me.

"Do you know anybody with the initials L.L?" I asked him.

He thought for a few moments.

"Laura Lyons," he told me at last. "Have you met a man called Frankland yet? He lives up on the moor, about four miles from here. Laura Lyons is his daughter. She married against his wishes, then her husband left her. She's had a pretty bad time, I hear. Jack Stapleton and Sir Charles have both tried to help her. They bought her a typewriter and she earns a living in Coombe Tracey."

I hurried back to Baskerville Hall for dinner. When Barrymore brought my coffee, I asked him if his brother-in-law was still on the moor.

"I think so, sir," he told me, "somebody's taken the food... unless it was the other man who took it."

I stared at Barrymore in surprise.

"You know that there is another man, then?" I asked.

"Yes, sir," Barrymore replied, "my brother-in-law told me. He's living in one of those old stone huts out there. A boy takes him food. I don't like it, Dr Watson – I tell you straight, sir, that I don't like it."

He stared out of the window at the rain-lashed moor.

"There's foul play out there somewhere," he whispered. "What's the stranger out there waiting for?

When Barrymore had gone, I walked over to the window and looked out. What must it be like out there on such a wild night? What hatred makes a man hide up there on the moor?

"I feel that he lies at the centre of this mystery," I told myself. "And tomorrow I shall find him!"

CHAPTER SIX

The Man on the Moor

I decided to visit Laura Lyons first.

She was sitting at her typewriter when I was shown to her room. I thought she was very beautiful, except for a hard look in her eyes.

"Why have you come here?" she asked coldly.

"It is about Sir Charles Baskerville," I replied. "You knew him, didn't you?"

"He was very kind to me," she said. "Without his help, I should have starved."

"Did you ever write to him?" I asked.

She looked at me with an angry gleam in her hazel eyes.

"Once or twice, to thank him for his kindness," she said at last.

"Did you ever write to Sir Charles asking him to meet you?" I asked.

Mrs Lyons looked angry again.

"Really, sir, this is a very strange question," she said.

"I am sorry, madam, but I must repeat it."

"Then I answer – certainly not," she said.

"Not on the very day of Sir Charles' death?" I asked.

The lady turned deadly pale. "No," she whispered.

"No."

"Please, please, as you are a gentleman, burn this letter, and be at the gate by ten o'clock," I said slowly.

She almost fainted as she heard my words.

"I did write that letter," she said quietly. "But I have no reason to be ashamed of it."

"What happened when you got there?" I asked her.

"I didn't go," she said. "You must believe me, I am telling the truth. When I heard about poor Sir Charles' death, I couldn't say anything. I was afraid that I would be blamed."

"I believe you," I said gently.

I left her and returned across the moor to Baskerville Hall. I stopped for a moment and stared at the huts dotted on the hillside.

"I shall go back to the place where I saw the man in the moonlight," I thought, "and then I'll explore every hut on the moor, until I find him."

I set off again. Good luck was with me, because on the way I met Laura's father, Frankland. I did not like him, but I stopped to talk. I wanted to find out as much as I could.

"I know where that escaped prisoner is," he told me excitedly. "I've seen a boy taking food to him every day."

"How do you know this?" I asked in surprise.

"You shall judge for yourself, sir!" he laughed. "I have

a fine telescope on the roof of my house!"

I followed Frankland eagerly and looked through his telescope. Sure enough, after a short time, I saw a small boy trudging slowly up a hill, close to where I had seen the man in the moonlight.

I made my excuses and left as soon as possible. The sun was already sinking when I reached the top of the hill. There was no sound and no movement anywhere, except for one silent bird in the air above me. I looked at the huts below me.

"Only one of them has a roof," I thought. "That is where the stranger must be hiding!"

I made my way slowly towards the hut, my heart thudding. I put my hand on my revolver and walked to the door. Then I looked quickly inside.

There was nobody there.

I stared at the pile of blankets, at the remains of food – then at a sheet of paper. I read:

"Dr Watson has gone to Coombe Tracey."

Was this man following me, not Sir Henry?

"I shall not leave this hut until I know," I thought.

I sat down in the dark hut and waited with growing terror. And then at last I heard him. Far away came the sharp clink of a boot hitting a stone. Then another and another, coming nearer and nearer. I shrank back.

A shadow fell across the opening of the hut.

CHAPTER SEVEN

The Net Closes In

"It is a lovely evening, my dear Watson," said a well-known voice. "I really think that you will be more comfortable outside than in."

For a moment or two, I sat breathless, hardly able to believe my ears. That cold, careful voice could only belong to one man in the world.

"Holmes!" I cried – "Holmes!"

"Come out," he said, "and please be careful with the revolver."

I went outside. Holmes was sitting on a stone. He looked thin and tired, but his face was bronzed by the sun and the wind. In his tweed suit and cap he looked like any other tourist visiting the moor.

"I was never more glad to see you," I said, shaking his hand.

"Or more astonished, eh?" he asked.

"Well, yes," I said.

"I am surprised, too," he told me, "I had no idea that you were on my trail, until I was almost inside the hut just now."

"You saw my footprint?" I asked.

"No, Watson," he replied, "I recognised your cigarette.

You threw it down when you ran into the hut. You saw me, no doubt, when you were looking for the prisoner? I was careless to stand outside when the moon was out."

"Yes, I saw you then," I told him. "Now your boy has been seen. That's how I found you."

Holmes picked up the scribbled note.

"So you have visited Mrs Laura Lyons?" he asked.

"Exactly," I said.

"Well done!" Holmes said. "We are both on the same track. When we put our results together, we shall have a fuller knowledge of the case."

"Well, I am glad that you are here," I said, "for the mystery of this case was becoming too much for me. But what have you been doing, Holmes? Don't you trust me? I think I deserve better!"

"My dear Watson," Holmes said, "please forgive me if I seem to have tricked you. But if I had come with you and Sir Henry, our enemies would have been on guard. As it is, I have been able to make enquiries in secret..."

"But why keep me in the dark?" I asked angrily.

"You would have tried to see me," Holmes replied. "It would have been a risk."

"My reports have all been wasted!" I cried, my voice trembling.

Holmes took a bundle of papers from his pocket.

"Here are your reports, my dear fellow," he said. "And very good they are, too. I must congratulate you on the intelligence you have shown in this most difficult case."

Holmes' praise drove the anger from my mind.

"You are right," I muttered.

"That's better," he said. "And now tell me the result of your visit to Mrs Laura Lyons. If you had not gone today, I should have gone tomorrow."

The sun had set and dusk was settling over the moor. The air had turned cold and we went back into the hut for warmth. I told him what I had learned at Coombe Tracey.

"This is most important," he said when I had finished. "It fills a gap. You are aware that there is also a close friendship between Mrs Lyons and Jack Stapleton. Now if I could use it to persuade Mr Stapleton's wife..."

"His wife?" I asked in surprise.

"I am giving you some information now, in return for all you have just given me," Holmes said. "The lady you think of as his sister is really his wife."

"Are you sure, Holmes?" I cried. "Then how could he let Sir Henry fall in love with her?"

"That does no harm to anybody – except Sir Henry," Holmes said. "Stapleton thought his wife would be more useful if everybody thought she was a free woman."

"It is Stapleton, then, who is our enemy – it is he who followed us in London after Sir Henry's arrival?" I asked.

"So I read the riddle," Holmes said.

"And the warning, the note to Sir Henry – it must have come from his wife?" I asked.

"Exactly," Holmes replied.

"But if this woman is his wife," I said, "where does Mrs Laura Lyons fit into the plan?"

"She expected to become his wife," Holmes said.

"And when she learns that Stapleton is already married...?" I asked.

"Then we may find the lady will want to help us," Holmes said. "Now, Watson, don't you think you have been away from Sir Henry too long? Your place should be at Baskerville Hall."

He stared straight into my eyes.

"Remember," he said, "Sir Henry is in great danger."

CHAPTER EIGHT

Murder on the Moor

The last rays of the sun had faded away. It was night now and a few stars twinkled in a dark purple sky. I got up.

"One last question, Holmes," I said. "What is Stapleton after?"

Holmes' voice dropped to a whisper.

"I only know that it is murder, Watson," he said, "cold-blooded murder. Do not ask me the reason, not yet. But my net is closing in on Stapleton, as he is closing in on Sir Henry. There is only one danger. He could strike before we are ready. I need another day or two. Until then, guard Sir Henry. I wish you had not left him for so long! I..."

Holmes suddenly stopped speaking.

"What's that?" he asked.

A terrible scream filled the air – a long scream of terror and horror. The terrible cry turned my blood cold.

"Oh, my God!" I gasped. "What is it? What does it mean?"

Holmes jumped to his feet and went to the door of the hut.

"Sssh!" he whispered. "Sssh!"

Now the cry was nearer, louder and more urgent than before.

"Where is it?" Holmes whispered.

I knew from his voice that he was very shaken.

"Where is it, Watson?" he asked again.

"There, I think," I said, pointing into the darkness.

The terrible cry swept through the silent night again, louder and nearer than ever.

"The hound!" Holmes cried. "Come, Watson, come! Let us hope we are not too late!"

Holmes started to run across the moor and I followed him. From the ground immediately in front of us came one last cry of despair, then a heavy thud. We stopped and listened. No sound broke the heavy silence of the still night.

I saw Holmes put his hand to his forehead. Then he stamped his foot on the ground.

"What if Stapleton has beaten us, Watson?" he said. "What if we are too late!"

"No, no, surely not!" I cried.

"I was a fool to wait!" Holmes cried.

We ran on through the darkness, forcing our way through bushes, stumbling on rocks towards the direction of those terrible cries. At every hill, Holmes looked around hopefully. But the shadows were thick on the moor and nothing moved.

"Listen, what's that?" I asked.

We heard a low moan. There it was again on our left!

On that side was a ridge of rocks which ended in a steep cliff. On the slope below, we could just make out a dark shape. As we ran towards it, we could make out the shape of a man. He was lying face down on the ground, his body hunched up. Not a whisper, not a sound came from his lips now.

Holmes bent down over the man and struck a match. In the light, we saw the crushed skull, a growing pool of blood seeping from it.

And it shone upon something else, something which made us feel sick and faint – the body of Sir Henry Baskerville!

CHAPTER NINE

A Strong Enemy

There could be no mistake. In the flickering light of the match, we caught a glimpse of the same tweed suit that Sir Henry had worn when he had first visited us in Baker Street. Suddenly, the match went out, and with it, all hope that we might have been wrong.

"The brute! The brute!" I cried. "Oh, Holmes, I shall never forgive myself for leaving him!"

"I am more to blame than you, Watson," Holmes said. "This is the biggest blow of my career."

"We heard his screams and could not save him!" I cried. "But where is this hound which drove him to his death? And Stapleton, where is he?"

"Now we have to prove the link between Stapleton and the hound," Holmes said. "We do not even know if the hound really exists. But Sir Henry obviously died trying to escape from it. Just as Sir Charles did."

We stood by that mangled body until the moon rose. Then we climbed to the top of the rocks over which our poor friend had fallen. We gazed over the shadowy moor, at the yellow light of Stapleton's house far in the distance.

"Let's seize him now!" I cried.

"No," Holmes said. "Now we must send for help to take back our dear friend."

Holmes looked at the body one last time.

"A beard! A beard! This man has a beard!" he shouted. "He is not Sir Henry!"

We turned the man over. There was no doubt. Lying in front of us was Mrs Barrymore's brother, the escaped prisoner.

"Sir Henry gave some of his clothes to Barrymore," I said. "He must have passed them on to his brother-in-law."

"The hound thought it was Sir Henry," Holmes said. "It must have been given something of Sir Henry's to sniff, to pick up the scent. Of course, the boot that went missing from Sir Henry's hotel in London. Do you remember?"

I nodded. As we talked, we saw a man approaching us across the moor.

"It's Stapleton!" Holmes whispered. "Not a word about our suspicions or my plan won't work."

Jack Stapleton stopped in surprise when he saw us.

"Why, Dr Watson," he said, "you are the last person I expected to see on the moor at this time of night."

He looked at the ground.

"Is somebody hurt?" he asked. "Not – don't tell me that it's our friend Sir Henry!"

Stapleton hurried past me and stooped over the body. I heard him take a deep breath and his cigar fell from his fingers. Then he looked up at us with a ghastly pale face as he tried to hide his surprise and disappointment.

"Who – who's this?" he stammered.

"An escaped prisoner," I explained.

"How… how did he die?" Stapleton asked.

"He appears to have fallen over these rocks and broken his neck," Holmes told him. "What brings you here, sir?"

"I heard a cry," Stapleton said at last. "I was afraid something had happened to Sir Henry. I asked him to dine with me tonight, and he has not arrived."

He smiled at Holmes.

"We have been expecting you, Mr Sherlock Holmes," he said.

Holmes bowed.

"I return to London tomorrow," he said coldly.

We left Stapleton there and set off to Baskerville Hall.

"What a nerve the man has!" Holmes exclaimed. "He is a strong enemy indeed! We are close to unmasking him, but…"

"Why can't we arrest him now?" I cried angrily.

"So far, we cannot prove anything!" Holmes said. "We should be laughed out of court. I hope Mrs Laura Lyons may help us. Now, say nothing to Sir Henry about tonight, Watson."

I looked at Holmes in surprise. He paused.

"Then he will be stronger for the terrible ordeal he will face tomorrow night."

CHAPTER TEN

The Hound of the Baskervilles

Sir Henry was pleased to see Sherlock Holmes and we talked for a long time of the strange events of the past few weeks. As we were eating dinner, I noticed that Holmes kept staring over my head at the wall behind me.

"Those are fine portraits, Sir Henry," he said at last. "Tell me, who is the man wearing black velvet and lace?"

"Ah, he is the cause of all the trouble," Sir Henry said. "That is the wicked Hugo Baskerville, who started the legend of the Hound of the Baskervilles."

Holmes stared at the portrait all evening. Later, when Sir Henry had gone to bed, he took me back to the dining-room and held a candle up to Hugo Baskerville's portrait.

"Is it like anyone you know?" he asked.

"There is something of Sir Henry about the jaw," I told him.

Holmes jumped onto a chair and put his arm over Hugo's hat and ringlets, to hide them.

"Good heavens!" I cried in amazement. "He could be Stapleton!"

"Stapleton is a Baskerville, I am sure of it," Holmes said. "This is our missing link, Watson. He is after his inheritance." Holmes laughed. "We have him, Watson, we have him. I swear that before tomorrow night he will be fluttering in our net as helpless as one of his butterflies!"

Early the next morning, Holmes told Sir Henry that he and I were leaving for London. Our friend looked deeply hurt.

"You must do as I tell you, Sir Henry," Holmes said. "You will go in your carriage to Stapleton's tonight, then send the driver back. Tell the Stapletons that you intend to walk home."

"Walk across the moor?" Sir Henry asked, horrified. "You told me never to do that!"

"You must do it tonight!" Holmes said. "You will be safe. Take your usual path."

"Then I will do it," Sir Henry replied.

At the railway station, we met the boy who had looked after Holmes so well on the moor. He caught the London train, with instructions to send a telegram as soon as he arrived – from Sherlock Holmes.

We went immediately to see Mrs Laura Lyons. When Holmes told her the truth about Stapleton's wife, she turned deadly pale.

"But he promised to marry me," she whispered. "Yes, I will help you, sir," she said at last.

"The letter to Sir Charles, that was Stapleton's idea?" Holmes asked.

"Yes," Mrs Lyons whispered. "Then he frightened me into not telling anybody."

"Thank you, Mrs Lyons," Holmes said. "That is all I need you to tell me."

We went straight up onto the moors when we left Mrs Lyons, walking slowly through a thick fog, which rolled in from Grimpen Mire. As we came close to Merripit House, I peeped through the dining room window and saw Jack Stapleton talking to Sir Henry. After a few minutes, he left the house and walked to a building in the grounds. He unlocked the door, went in for a minute, then came out, locking the door again.

I went back to the others. A thick white fog drifted towards us, like a shimmering icefield. But above us, the sky was clear.

"Sir Henry must come out before the fog reaches us," Holmes whispered.

The fog curled over the roof of Merripit House towards us. We moved back a little and the fog came after us. Suddenly, the sound of footsteps broke the silence of the moor. Sir Henry came through the curtain of fog, into the clear, starlit night. Then I sprang to my feet, trying not to scream.

A dreadful shape had sprung from the shadow of the fog. It was a hound – but nothing like anything I had ever seen before. Fire burst from its open mouth, its eyes glowed and flames flickered along its nose.

I had never seen anything so hellish and so savage.

That huge black creature leaped along the path after our dear friend. We hesitated, Holmes and I, then we fired our pistols at it. The creature gave a terrible howl, but it did not stop. We saw Sir Henry look behind him, his face white in the moonlight. He raised his hands in horror.

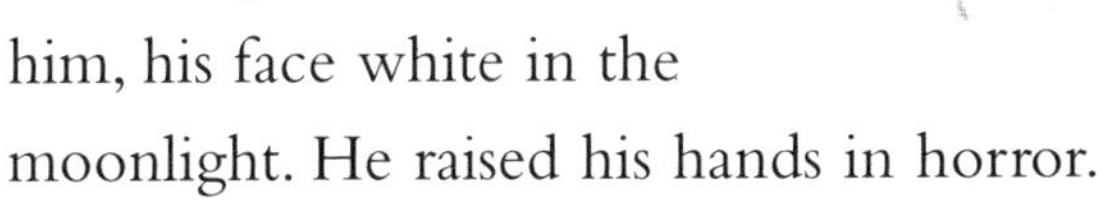

"If we can wound the hound, we can kill it!" Holmes shouted as he ran after the creature.

Sir Henry screamed . The hound roared, then leaped upon his victim. At that moment, Holmes fired five times. With a last roll of agony, the animal rolled onto its back, then lay still. The giant hound was dead.

"My God," Sir Henry whispered. "What was it?"

"It's dead, whatever it was," Holmes said. "We've laid the family ghost for ever."

We looked at the dead creature in front of us. It was

as large as a lioness. Even now, its jaws seemed to drip with a bluish flame. Its small, deep-set cruel eyes had a ring of fire around them. I put my hand on the hound's glowing nose, then took my hand away. Now my hand gleamed in the darkness.

"Phosphorus!" I said.

Sir Henry staggered to his feet, pale and trembling. He went and sat on a rock, shivering.

"We must leave you now," Holmes told him, "we still have to catch our man. We shall look first in Merripit House!"

But we found only one person there – Jack Stapleton's wife, tied and gagged and bruised.

"There is only one place he could have gone," she told us when she could speak at last. "There is an old tin mine on an island in the middle of Grimpen Mire. He kept his hound there. But nobody could find his way there in this fog – except him."

"We shall wait until morning," Holmes said.

We went back to Sir Henry and took him to Baskerville Hall. The news of Stapleton's crimes was a great blow to him, and he fell ill with a fever.

Holmes and I went into Grimpen Mire the next morning. There we found Sir Henry's missing boot and a tin of phosphorus.

But we never found Jack Stapleton's body.